Pop's Cookie Duster

story by **Don & Lee Doyle**

illustrations by **Annette Deheyes**

#new texture

A New Texture book

copyright © 2016 Don and Lee Doyle

Cover art by Annette Debevec

Editorial consultant: Sandee Curry/SandeeCurry.com

Book design and layout by Wyatt Doyle

www.PopsCookieDuster.com

www.NewTexture.com

Authors' Acknowledgements

Thanks to Sadie Schauerman, Annie Schauerman, Sharon McMahon, Clayton Doyle, and Victoria Doyle

Artist's Acknowledgements

Julie Lonneman, for her artistic mentoring
Evelyn, Audrey, and Charlotte Debevec, who modeled for their Grammy

ISBN 978-1-943444-48-9

First New Texture softcover edition: April 2016

Also available in hardcover and as an ebook

Printed in the United States of America

10 9 8 7 6 5 4 3 2 1

For Liam and James —
I hope you enjoy my book!
Annette Debevec

To our grandchildren
and future grandchildren

My name is Daisy and I am 6 years old.

My sister's name is Juliana. She is 4 years old.

Daddy has a surprise for us!

Pop is coming to visit!

Pop is Daddy's Daddy.

Some people call him Granddad, or Popi, or Pop Pop.

We call him Pop.

He has to take an airplane to visit us.

He brings our grandmother, too.

We call her Mom Mom. We could call her Gran, or
Nonna, or Nana, but she likes Mom Mom the best.

Mom Mom likes to help us put puzzles together.

When I was little, the puzzles had big pieces.

Now that I am 6, the puzzles have small pieces.

We like to play Bingo with Mom Mom.

She lets us use candy for markers.

We get to eat the candy when we finish playing.

Ophelia the cat likes to lie in the sun
on our bedroom floor.

We wish Mom Mom and Pop lived closer to us
so we could play with them every day.

The last time they visited, Daddy said to Pop,
"I see you brought your Cookie Duster."

"I never go anywhere without it," laughed Pop.

"What's a Cookie Duster?" I asked.

"Maybe you'll find out later," said Pop.

Daddy and Pop are funny. They should be clowns. They like to play tricks on us and tell jokes. We laugh a lot when Pop is here with Daddy.

It was raining that day. We were sad. We like to play outside.

Pop saw our sad faces, but he had a big smile on his face.

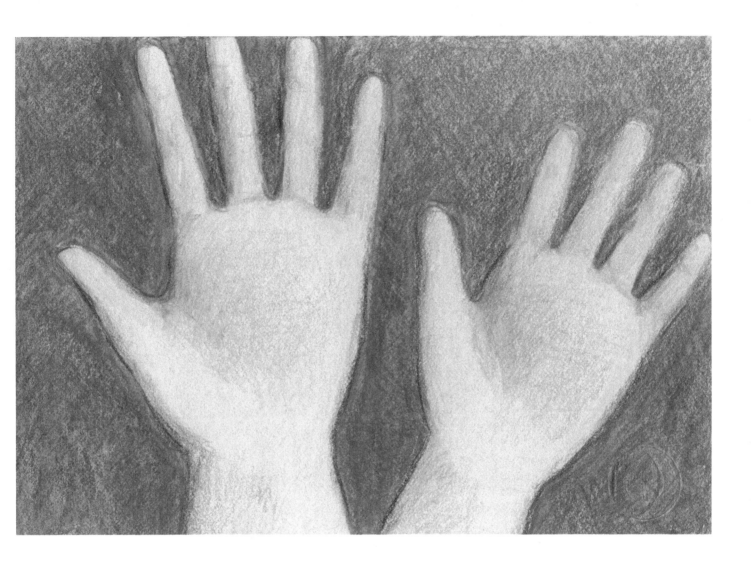

Pop asked, "Who wants to have fun?"

"We do! We do! We do!"

"OK, but I need help," he said.

Pop walked into the kitchen.

"Where is the oatmeal?"

"Pop, oatmeal is for breakfast."

"Not today, Juliana."

"Pop, are you playing a joke on us?"

"Let's get to work," said Pop.

He opened all the cabinets and picked out
lots of stuff.

He put butter and sugar in a bowl.

Pop put Juliana on the counter.

I got a stool and sat next to Pop.

Pop started putting more things into the bowl.

He put flour on my nose.

Juliana said, "Me too! Me too!"

Soon it was time to stir the bowl. Pop said we needed to mix everything together.

"We need a cookie sheet," Pop said.

Yay, cookies!

"We need two spoons to finish," said Pop.

I got a spoon, and I passed one to Juliana.

"Put the spoon in the dough, take it out, and use the other spoon to push it off," explained Pop.

We made neat rows of dough on the cookie sheet.

Pop put the cookies into the oven.

We had to wait a long time for them to cook.

At last, Pop opened the oven.

All we could smell was warm cookies.

I put my tongue out and began to lick the air.

Pop slid the cookies onto the counter to cool. As we looked at the cookies, I saw something red.

"Pop, what are the red things?"

"Oh, that is my secret ingredient...cranberries!"

Pop looked at the cookies and picked up the two biggest ones.

He gave one to me and the other to Juliana.

"Don't eat the cookies yet," Pop said. "I have to test them with my Cookie Duster."

"What's a Cookie Duster?" I said.

"I'll show you," answered Pop.

Pop took a bite of my cookie. With a twinkle in his
eye and a wiggle of his whiskers, a piece was gone.
A big smile appeared on his face.

"I call my mustache a Cookie Duster," said Pop,
"and this cookie passed the test. It is OK to eat."

"Pop, I think you are playing a trick on us," I said.

Pop just laughed, and we ate our cookies.

Yum, yum! The cookies tasted so good. The secret ingredient was a tasty surprise.

We always have fun with Mom Mom and Pop.

Even if it rains, we still have a good time.

We love when our Mom Mom and Pop visit us.

POP'S SPECIAL OATMEAL COOKIE RECIPE

Preparation time: 20 minutes   Cook time: 8 minutes

- 1 cup (2 sticks) soft butter
- 1 ¼ cup firmly packed brown sugar
- 2 eggs
- 1 teaspoon vanilla
- 1 ½ cups all-purpose flour
- 1 teaspoon baking soda
- ½ teaspoon salt
- 3 cups old fashioned oats, uncooked
- 1 cup dried, sweetened cranberries

Preheat oven to 350°F. In a large bowl, beat butter and sugar until creamy. Beat in eggs and vanilla. In a medium bowl, stir together flour, baking soda, and salt. Beat gradually into butter mixture. Add oats and cranberries, mix just until combined.

Drop dough in tablespoons onto ungreased cookie sheets.

Bake 8 to 10 minutes or until golden brown.

Cool slightly on cookie sheets. Place cookies on a plate to cool completely.

Makes 3 dozen.

new texture

CPSIA information can be obtained
at www.ICGtesting.com
Printed in the USA
BVOW10s2055110316

440080BV00006B/6/P